**MINDSCAPE**
PAGES

A BIG AND WARM THANK YOU FOR CHOOSING
**Mindscape PAGES** !

WE HOPE YOU HAD A LOVELY TIME USING THS
COLORING BOOK?

It would be of great help
if you could leave us a
review! We welcome your
feedback, as our main
goal is to create products
that YOU LOVE!

Like this book?

Scan me!